NOW YOU CAN READ....
The Elves and the Shoemaker

STORY ADAPTED BY LUCY KINCAID
ILLUSTRATED BY GILLIAN EMBLETON

BRIMAX BOOKS • CAMBRIDGE • ENGLAND

Once there was a shoemaker. He sat at his bench making shoes all day long. He worked very hard but nobody would pay him a fair price for the shoes he made. He and his wife were very poor.

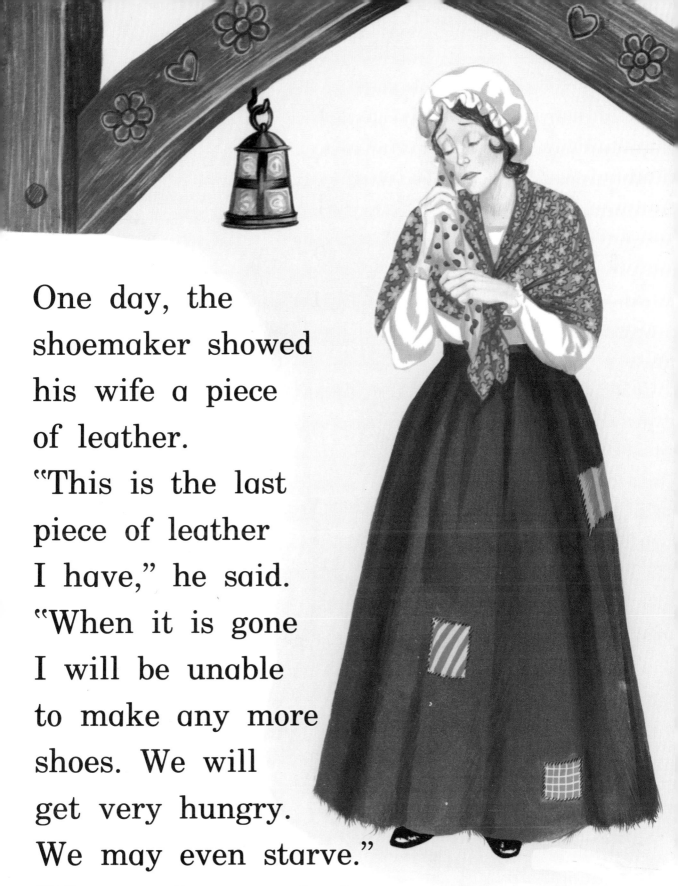

One day, the
shoemaker showed
his wife a piece
of leather.
"This is the last
piece of leather
I have," he said.
"When it is gone
I will be unable
to make any more
shoes. We will
get very hungry.
We may even starve."
"No wonder you look so sad," said
his wife. She was sad herself.

The shoemaker cut out the pieces
for the last pair of shoes. He
put them on the bench.
"It is late," he said. "Let us
go to bed. I will sew the pieces
together in the morning."

"Wife! Wife!" he called loudly next morning. "Come quickly!"
"What is it?" cried his wife. She ran into the workshop. There on the bench was a beautiful pair of finished shoes.
"Did you get up in the night and make them?" she asked.
The shoemaker shook his head.
"Then how did they get there?" she asked.
"I do not know," said the shoemaker

"Whoever made the shoes meant us to have them," said the shoemaker. "They would not have left them behind otherwise."

He took the shoes to market. He sold them for a very good price. He and his wife would not starve that day, or the next.

When the shoemaker had bought food, he had enough money left to buy leather for TWO more pairs of shoes.

He cut the pieces for the new shoes and laid them on the bench. "I will sew them tomorrow," he said.

"Wife! Wife! Come quickly!" called the shoemaker next morning. "It has happened again!"

"I don't believe it!" said the shoemaker's wife. There, on the bench, were two pairs of finished shoes.

"Look how well they are made," said the shoemaker. "There isn't a stitch out of place."

"Fine shoes for sale!" he cried when he got to the market place. "Fine shoes for sale!"

He sold both pairs in the first five minutes he was there. He was paid a very good price for them too. That day he bought enough leather to make four more pairs of shoes.

And so it went on. Every night the shoemaker left pieces of leather on the bench. Every morning they had been sewn into shoes. Every day he bought more leather.

One day, the shoemaker's wife said, "I do wish we knew who is making the shoes for us. We owe everything to them. I would like to say thank you."

"I know how we can find out," said the shoemaker.

That night he put the pieces of leather on the bench as before. He put out the light, as before. But instead of going to bed, as before, the shoemaker and his wife hid in the darkest corner of the room and waited. At midnight two little elves stepped in through the open window.

They sat cross-legged on the bench
and began to sew. They did not
waste a minute. When they had put
the last stitch into the last shoe
they slipped away as quietly as
they had come.

The shoemaker and his wife hurried to the window.

"We must find a way of thanking them," said the shoemaker.

"The poor little things," said his wife. "Did you notice how ragged their clothes were? And did you notice they had no shoes?"

"I will make them shoes," said the shoemaker.

"And I will make them each a set of clothes," said his wife.

The shoemaker took the finest, softest piece of leather he had, and made two pairs of tiny shoes. He had never made anything so small before.

The shoemaker's wife took the finest cloth she could find and made two sets of tiny clothes. She knitted two pairs of tiny stockings. She made two tiny hats. She had never made anything quite so small before.

By Christmas Eve everything was ready. That night the shoemaker put all the shoe leather underneath the bench. On top of the bench he put the two pairs of tiny shoes. His wife laid the two sets of tiny clothes beside them. Then they hid and waited for the elves to come.

When the elves saw what was on the bench they cried out in delight. "These must be for us!" they said. They took off their rags and dressed themselves in their new clothes. They put on their new shoes. They put on their new hats. And all the time they smiled and smiled.

The two happy little elves danced
a merry jig all along the bench.
"Now we are no longer poor,
Cobbling we will do no more,"
they sang.
Then they skipped out through the
window and were gone.

The shoemaker and his wife never saw the elves again. But their luck had changed. The shoes the shoemaker made, sold as well as the shoes the elves had made. They were never poor again and lived happily ever after.

All these appear in the pages of
the story. Can you find them?

shoemaker

shoemaker's wife

shoes

bench